MYSTERY AT WASHTE
KATHLEEN MARTIN

For Single Mothers Everywhere

For Single Mothers Everywhere

ACKNOWLEDGMENTS
I would like to acknowledge the guidance and support of the Central Phoenix Writing Workshop

CHAPTER 1

My name is Alice Birdwhistle. I'm 34 years old and live in Washte, a small town thirty miles north of Lincoln, Nebraska. I quit high school when I got pregnant, but I like to call myself "self-taught." I've read weird but important books like "Ulysses." And I try to learn ten new words a day. I'm currently working on an online degree in Greek mythology. How does a degree in Greek mythology help with my job at the Quick Trip, which includes cleaning out the Slurpee machine? I'm not sure yet.

Washte is the Lakota word for "Good," but that doesn't stop bad things from happening here. Couples cheating on each other, shoplifting at Wal-Mart, fistfights at barbeques after the beer had flowed too freely, and three months ago, Joan, my next-door neighbor, went missing.

The consensus amongst most Washteans I spoke with was that Eric, Joan's husband, had killed her. Of course, most Washteans are big fans of murder mystery shows like *Dateline* and *48 Hours*, where the spouse is always the killer.

I believe I was the last person to see Joan before she disappeared. It was just after 2 PM on Halloween Eve. I'm sure of that time because I was returning home from the Washte Quick Trip job. Our homes are semi-detached, so we share a common driveway. Just as I pulled into the drive, Joan was exiting her house. She was wearing a jacket with the hood pulled over her head, which was a little strange.

She'd never worn a hoodie before, even when it was freezing. Now I wonder if she was trying to disguise herself, but why and from whom?

I lowered the car window and yelled, "Happy Halloween!"

"Happy Halloween," Joan yelled back but gave me this weird smile and hurried past her car, which was even stranger. Joan never walked anywhere. Plus, there was that peculiar smile, which was too forced, maybe even fearful.

Eric dutifully reported her missing, but, nevertheless, he became the prime suspect or, as Sheriff Carton was quoted in the local newspaper, "a person of interest." But so far, nothing's come up to link Eric to Joan's disappearance.

I tried to contact Eric to express my condolences, but all I got was his answering machine, and he never returned my calls. Why is he avoiding me?

I want to believe that I'm not quick to judge, but I wouldn't be surprised if he had something to do with Joan's disappearance. I know "something to do with" sounds a little vague. I'll be more direct. Did he kill her? That sounds too precise. All I know for sure is that I've never liked him. His face is permanently set in an arrogant smirk like he's looking down at me, even though we're the same height - 5'6".

Where most Washteans wear high tops, Eric wears those tasseled loafers, like he's trying to be way more sophisticated than everyone else, but Gracie, my fourteen-year-old daughter, says they make him look "way not cool."

He told me he was in his thirties, but wasn't specific. I'd say he looks more in his 40's or even 50's.

I heard him interviewed on TV about Joan's disappearance, and he said something that I thought was peculiar. He said that Joan had been "reasonably fine" when he saw her at breakfast the morning she went missing.

Reasonably fine? That sounded unfinished to me. He should have come clean with something like, "Joan was reasonably fine considering that her life with me was pure hell." Of course, those would be my words, not his.

Sheriff Carton interviewed me a few months after Joan vanished. Carton had taken over the investigation after Sherriff Johnson had retired. Johnson only did a half-assed investigation before his retirement. I guess he didn't think the case warranted any further work, or he just couldn't be bothered chasing down, as he put it, "a stray wife."

The former and current sheriffs were complete opposites. Johnson had an overhanging beer belly and ever-present food stains on his shift.

Carton was square-jawed, fit and trim, with ice-blue eyes and a military buzz cut. His badge was pinned to his freshly ironed shirt. He's definitely not my type, but then why am I even telling you that.

When I told Carton about Eric's comment and Joan's weird smile, he gave me this "so what?" look. Sherriff Carton and Eric seem to be cut from the same cloth - both arrogant assholes.

Am I turning into a man-hater?

Possibly.

Sherriff Carton asked me if I'd ever heard Joan and Eric fighting, or had Joan ever confided in me that she was afraid of Eric, or had he threatened her.

I had never heard them fighting, and Joan had never confided in me about anything. Most of our conversations stayed in the safe confines of the weather or the obligatory-but-never-truly-answered-how-are-you-I'm-fine exchange. But there was one exception. It happened a week before her disappearance, but I was too embarrassed to tell Carton about it.

It was just after midnight. I'd spent the day sweeping cockroaches and dead mice out of the Quick Trip storeroom - an even lower point in my very low-point job. I was depressed and miserable. I couldn't get to sleep. I came out on my front porch to have a cigarette and cry. The street looked as deserted as our suburb could be at midnight, but I wasn't alone. Joan must have been on her porch too and heard my sobs because she came over and sat down next to me.

I tried to wipe my tears on my sleeve, but she put her hand on my arm to stop me.

"Go ahead and cry if you want to," she said. "There's nothing wrong with crying. Of course, if you'd rather be alone, that's okay too. I can go."

I usually do my crying in private, but there was such a comfort in Joan's voice, I didn't want her to leave.

We sat together in silence for a good two minutes, which is a very long time for me. Typically any lull in a conversation produces sharp anxiety in me that has to be calmed immediately by some pointless comment.

"You really don't have to stay out here with me. I'll be fine," I said, hoping she wouldn't leave.

"You didn't sound fine."

We both laughed. I rarely find my own brand of off-beat humor, but it's very important on how comfortable I can be with someone. "I guess I'm just feeling down about my crummy job," I said. "I should get a better one."

"What's stopping you?" she asked not as a criticism but more as an encouragement.

"I don't know. I guess I've never had much ambition. I never finished high school, and I take these silly online courses that never amount to anything. I'm just so unfocused. I'm sorry, I must sound like such a loser. I should've stayed in school. I should've---"

"Sorry, but I have to stop you. Getting an education is important but nowhere near as important as self-confidence. You don't need an education for that. You just need to believe in yourself."

I wanted to talk more, but I ended up crying again. She put her arm around me and hugged me.

"Don't ever apologize for your feelings about anything."

Joan boosted my spirits a little that night, but now I'm convinced she needed help too. I was too caught up in my own problems to ask about hers, but maybe she wouldn't have felt comfortable confiding in me. She was an English professor at the University of Omaha; I worked at the Quick Trip.

She is what I want to be: educated, sophisticated, confident, and trim. I could lose twenty pounds - no, make that thirty. I always tried to impress her by using words like "dutifully," and she seemed dutifully impressed but only dutifully like she knew I was trying to impress her and regarded it as rather pathetic, or maybe I'm just assuming all that.

It was assumed by most Washteans that Joan just "Up and took off." I couldn't buy that. Something happened to her.

CHAPTER 2

It's Christmas Eve, approximately three months since Joan disappeared. I was doing some last-minute shopping at Walmart. Even though my presents were all wrapped, I was rummaging through a bin of discounted Christmas wrapping paper. Living on a very limited budget, I'm always in search of a bargain, even if it's a year ahead. For some reason, I looked up and saw a woman pass by. She was wearing the same jacket Joan wore the night she disappeared with the hood up.

I just saw a glimpse of the woman's face, but I was convinced it was Joan. I dropped all the wrapping paper I was holding back into the bin and started following the woman. She turned down an aisle. The aisle was crammed with shoppers when I finally managed to move past them. The woman had disappeared.

It made no sense that it was Joan. Why would she be walking around Wal-Mart on Christmas Eve? My over-active imagination kicked into high gear. It was Joan's apparition, which could only mean one thing. She was dead.

***

"How come all these friggin' lights don't work?" Bambi asked as soon as I walked through the door. She was standing next to our fake Christmas tree, holding a tumbleweed of colored lights. She's a short woman built like a sumo wrestler. She's been my stepmother for over ten years.

There's a hint of tobacco smoke in the air. We both smoke, but the house rule is to smoke outside.

"Were you smoking in here?" I asked.

"Gracie's downstairs," she answered.

Gracie is my 13-going-on-30-year-old daughter. She, Bambi, and I all live together under the same roof, or at least try to.

"That's not the point; we made a deal that––"

"Here, you do it then." She dropped the mangled ball of lights at my feet and headed to the door.

Bambi's temper is even shorter than mine. The last time we trimmed the tree together was a complete catastrophe. It started with hanging tinsel. She threw it in clumps onto the tree, whereas I placed one tinsel carefully over the end of each branch. She called me a "tight-assed bitch," and I called her a "worn-out douchebag." She swung at me, and I pushed her back into the tree, sending it crashing to the floor with her on top of it. There's no worse sight than a fallen Christmas tree crushed under the weight of a sumo wrestler.

Of course, the fight between Bambi and me wasn't about tree decorating. For ten years, it was an ongoing battle between two alpha females living under the same roof, with the same man, my father. She thought he spoiled me. I thought he spoiled her. He had to cash in all his retirement savings to pay off her gambling debt because the people she had borrowed from threatened to cut off her hands. The stress became too much for him, and one day while working on his car, he had a heart attack in the garage and died.

I found him.

The war between Bambi and me escalated after my dad's death because I accused her of causing it, which was the worst thing I could've said. She loved him just as much as I did. But grief can harden into anger faster than anything.

Despite her deep-rooted hostility towards me, she made an extraordinary gesture when I threatened to move out. She put the ownership of the house, which was mortgage-free thanks to my dad, in my name because she worried she'd put it all down on Black Jack. Her only request was that she be allowed to live in the house until, as she put it, "You kill me, or I die of natural causes."

This will be my first Christmas without my dad. No wonder Bambi's more bitchy than usual, but so am I. I'm not perfect, but at least I don't have a gambling addiction. My vices are minor, like smoking and pushing the spout on my box of Chianti a few too many times.

As I tried to untangle the Christmas tree lights, I suddenly got a whiff of "Shower-To-Shower," which smelt like baby powder with a punch to it. My dad used it all the time. Not only was I "seeing dead people," but I smelled them too.

Having my dad's spirit around me was too painful. I wanted him real.

"Get lost," I whispered. "Unless you can tell me the winning lottery numbers."

The smell evaporated. I must have made him angry, or perhaps I was going off the deep end, or maybe I've never come out of it.

CHAPTER 3

Gracie appeared from her hang-out in the basement as I was untangling the Christmas lights.

"What ya get at Wal-Mart?" she asked with a coy smile.

"How'd you know I was at Wal-Mart?" I told Bambi not to tell her where I was.

"Bambi told me. I hope you didn't get Justin Bieber. He's such a wanksta." She idolized Beiber last week, so I bought her "Believe" for Christmas. Are most thirteen-year-olds this fickle?

"Was Bambi smoking in the house?"

"No," Gracie answered with wide-eyed honesty, a sure sign she was lying. She adored Bambi and would never betray her.

For all I know, they were smoking together.

"Can I have my allowance in advance, or nobody's gonna get shit for Christmas."

"Please don't use that kind of language."

"You use it."

"Not when I was your age." That was a lie. *I must stop lying to her.*

"Yeah, I bet. So can I have my allowance now?"

I wasn't sure whether to pursue the language lecture or just give her her allowance.

"Did you vacuum the upstairs?"

"Yeah, and cleaned the bathrooms – why do I have to do all the shit work around here?"

"The deal was that you'd get more allowance for cleaning the bathrooms."

"Well, I'm not cleaning them anymore."

"Fine, then you'll get less allowance."

"Fine." She held out her hand.

"Fine," I said, handing over her allowance.

She slid into her denim jacket. I noticed a decal on the back of it that wasn't there yesterday – a marijuana leaf.

Is she smoking pot now? Oh God, she's too young. I waited until I was seventeen. "Hey, what's that about?"

She went out the door without answering.

I haven't had a joint in over fourteen years, but I sure wish I had one now.

The truth is Gracie would not be here if it wasn't for marijuana. I bought my first doobie from our high school dealer and shared it with Matt, Gracie's soon-to-be father, in the back of Matt's father's Ford Taurus. Otis Redding's *These Arms of Mine* was playing on the radio, so the music and the marijuana broke down all my reservations about going all the way.

As fate would have it, seconds after I lost my virginity, I became pregnant.

Unbeknownst to Matt, his wealthy parents made me a proposition. If I signed a statement claiming That Matt was not the father (so he could get into West Point,) I would get a thousand bucks. I was so easily bought off. My dad never knew about that deal. I was too ashamed to tell him.

But I changed my mind. I would give the money back and tell Matt what had happened, but fate took an awful turn for the worse. He and his parents were killed in a head-on collision in the car in which Gracie was conceived in.

My pregnancy put a stop to my dad's dream of me going to college. He tried so hard to set me on the right path, but I was determined to follow my own reckless course.

My dad was a diehard New Yorker but chose to move to Nebraska after winning custody of me when I was nine. He wanted a safer, more wholesome environment to raise me in - so much for that plan.

Washte High was ripe with sex and drugs of all kinds.

My mom left him to pursue her acting career. She took my eight-year-old self with her until too many rejections and vodka shots got the better of her. Children's Aid returned me to my dad. He went through two more wives by the time I was 18. His second wife was a serious cokehead (as if there is a casual kind), and then Bambi, his third wife, was a serious gambler.

I guess my dad was addicted to addicts. It cost him everything.

I guess I'm more affected by Joan's disappearance than I realize. I kept wondering if that really was her at Walmart's?

And if it was, what made her come back?

Perhaps the truth is that I keep thinking about her because it takes my mind off my own life. My dad's death and Joan's disappearance have someone who made me really look at where I'm at, and where I'm at is not where I want to be. I want to disappear too, or start over again with a new life, where my mom wasn't an alcoholic, and I didn't get pregnant when I was 16. But obviously, that's not going to happen.

I'm stuck with the life I have right now.

I've got to get ready for Christmas regardless of how shitty I know it's going to be.

I wondered if there was any wine left in my box of Chianti and went into the kitchen to find out.

That night I decorated the tree by myself.

CHAPTER 4

I was adding that little packet of orange stuff to a pot of Kraft Dinner when I heard a sharp knock at the front door. I dreaded the urgency of that knock. Had something happened to Gracie? The doorbell rang with even greater persistence.

"You gettin' that!" Bambi yelled from upstairs.

Why does she make me face every possible catastrophe alone? I took in a deep breath and walked to the front door. The top of a man's bald head was visible through the door's transom. He wasn't wearing a policeman's cap. I relaxed a bit and opened the door.

Eric stood before me. It was the first time I'd seen him since Joan disappeared. He had undergone a transformation. He'd shaved his head, sprayed on a tan, looked twenty pounds lighter, and there was a diamond stud in his left ear.

A woman stood next to him. She looked fiftyish, but her skin was as taut as a china doll. Her long hair cascaded stylishly over one shoulder, and an earring the size of a hula hoop was suspended over the other.

"I'm sorry to bother you, but we have to talk. May we come in?" He looked very solemn and tense.

"Sure," I said and invited them into my living room.

Our fully loaded Christmas tree now stood leaning slightly to the left, surrounded by a clutter of empty boxes and wrinkled newspapers.

"Sorry for the mess. We just finished decorating the tree...I mean, I just finished decorating it...I mean, I did it last night." I was trying not to sound nervous and forced myself to laugh, which sounded even worse. "Can I get you anything?"

Eric shook his head, but his lady friend piped up, "Scotch rocks, please."

A trace of disapproval swept across Eric's face, but he patted her hand comfortingly. "I guess I could use something too."

"I was just having a glass of Chianti, or would you prefer scotch?"

"Scotch." Her voice was low and abrupt like she needed that drink fast.

"For me too," said Eric.

The woman gave him a slight jab in the ribs with her elbow.

"Oh, sorry," Eric said with a sheepish grin, "This is Angela, my assistant."

Angela grimaced but reached out to shake my hand. "I'm his *girlfriend*." She had a sharp jumpy handshake which was a little frightening.

Eric looked even more uncomfortable, "She was my assistant but has since become my friend."

"As in *girlfriend*," Angela insisted.

My mind raced with questions piling on top of each other. Did they see *each other before Joan went missing? Is that why she left? Is that why Eric killed her! Or maybe Angela killed her!*

"Angela has been helping me with Joan's disappearance. I mean, *deal* with her disappearance. We met after it happened."

"I was working for you *long* before Joan disappeared," said Angela. Her smile tightened. She was determined to set the record straight, and my suspicions of her harming Joan evaporated.

Eric's tone sharpened. "I know, I know, but I meant that you helped me deal with her disappearance after she disappeared."

"Well, obviously. How else could I---"

"I'll just go and get the scotch." I hoped my interruption gave them a chance to cool off. I stopped at the door. "Sorry, I just remembered, we don't have any scotch." In fact, we never had scotch. I couldn't afford it.

"Never mind. We don't need anything," said Eric. "We just came over to reconnect with you and to let you know that we're leaving today for a trip to the Bahamas. We'll be spending Christmas and New Year's there, and would you mind just putting our mail inside?"

"No, not at all."

"Here's the house key," he said.

I took the key from him, and he surprised me with a stiff hug. "Thanks, Alice, for all your help."

"You're welcome, but I really haven't done anything. I mean, I did call you and left messages but------

"Yeah, I got them. And I should've called you back."

"Oh, no, that's okay. You must have been overwhelmed by everything."

"He was overwhelmed by "Johnny Walker," said Angela.

At first, I didn't understand who the "Johnny Walker" Angela was referring to, but I caught on immediately when she made a drinking motion with her hand.

Eric looked embarrassed, and for the first time, I felt a particular empathy for him.

Gone was that smug smirk, and it was replaced with a look of guilt. Guilt about what, though? I wanted to tell him about seeing Joan at Wal-Mart, but under the circumstances with Angela there, it would have just stirred up more stuff that maybe was better left unstirred.

"Well, I hope you two have a great vacation."

"Thanks," said Eric. "And thanks for all your help."

"Sure." I wasn't sure of what help I had provided, but we all shook hands on it.

Bambi stood at the bottom of the stairs giving Eric and Angela the once-over as they passed by her to the door.

"Who's Mr. Clean?" asked Bambi after they left.

"Didn't you recognize him? That's Eric, Joan's husband.

"Man, has she changed."

"That *wasn't* Joan. That was his friend. Don't you remember? Joan's been missing for three months now."

"So he gets rid of his wife, has a makeover, and gets his mistress to move in?"

"What do you mean "gets rid" of?"

"You know what I mean, so quit pussyfooting around it."

I *did* know what she meant, but I wasn't about to say it out loud.

"Never mind. It's Christmas Eve. Let's you and me go outside and smoke and sing carols," I said.

For as long as I've known her, Bambi has never wanted to sing anything, let alone Christmas Carols. Nothing's normal anymore, but then when was it ever normal.

CHAPTER 5

No matter how grown-up I try to feel, I still have that childlike rush of excitement on Christmas morning. My mother never gave me what I'd ask for, and my dad just gave me cash. Can't go wrong with the cash, right? But I still hold up hope that Christmas will give me the present I've wished for. This Christmas I got a new mop from Bambi and a gift certificate for Mr. Submarine from Gracie.

I remember when Gracie made her presents for me: a plate painted with a large purple turkey, and a drawing of me with a smile that took up most of my face, to name just a few. Those days are gone.

I had maxed out my credit card on gifts for them: perfume, clothes, jewelry, a framed photograph of us all together smiling, but nothing seemed appreciated. Am I trying to buy their affection? Am I trying to change them into something they're not? Am I becoming a mean-spirited person? Yes, but I don't care. I'm angry.

After the gifts were opened, Gracie retreated to her bedroom on Planet Facebook and Bambi went outside for a cigarette. I was left alone with a mess of torn wrapping paper.

If only dad was here. He'd make everything right again.

Feeling right was up to me now, which was probably the way it should've been all along.

I invited Uncle Ted, my dad's brother, and Ted's fourth wife, Cindy, for Christmas dinner. Cindy is five years younger than me so I can't bring myself to call her "Aunt Cindy."

Even though Uncle Ted is the only other family I have, and even though I only see him and Cindy, once a year at Christmas, I always dread seeing him, and now that dad's not here, it's going to be even worse because he looks so much like my dad, but isn't like him in any way.

Uncle Ted is always carefully groomed and tailored whereas my dad wore jeans and stained t-shirts. My dad had one pair of shoes, brown hush puppies, and one gray suit which he wore to his high school graduation, fifty years ago.

Uncle Ted lived like a Saudi prince with a closet full of Savile Row suits, regular manicures, pedicures, facials, and his personal barber who not only cut his hair but also colored it an alarming red. Outside of a circus clown, who has bright red hair like that when they're over sixty?

My dad worked in the rough and dirty world of construction. Ted was a professional gambler. In fact, that's how my dad met Bambi. He joined Ted on a Vegas weekend and met Bambi at the Black Jack table. How romantic.

Ted's wife Cindy is a dancer, who worked at Caesar's Place. They met in a Vegas coffee shop. She was fresh off the bus from Idaho, with dreams of becoming a showgirl. She thought their costumes were "totally awesome" especially those "freakin' feathers." Ted paid for everything Cindy needed altered or enhanced to get her in the show.

Gracie thought their relationship was disgusting, and there was a time I would have agreed with her. I've since altered my opinion about women getting bodywork done for business. If men are willing to pay a lot of money to see manufactured body parts, who is exploiting whom?

I was called a "rabid feminist" by a man I dated once just because I told him he didn't have to stand up every time I left the table. I think he was just trying to be polite and I humiliated him. I think that's why the relationships I've had with men never lasted longer than a few months. Perhaps I am a "rabid feminist."

Bambi came into the kitchen to oversee everything while I was making the turkey stuffing. We got into a debate about where to cook the stuffing: inside the turkey or on top of the stove. I told her that research showed cooking it on the stove prevents salmonella poisoning.

"I've been on this planet for over 60 years, and I've been eatin' god damn turkey stuffing that's been cooked in the god damn turkey for every single one of those years, and ain't I still alive?" she asked.

"Don't swear like that - especially when Gracie might hear," I answered.

"Me? Ain't you heard yourself? Ain't you heard her?"

She made me feel slightly hypocritical, or maybe more than slightly. "At least I don't say 'ain't.'"

"Ain't nuthin' wrong with 'ain't'. 'It don't mean a thing if it ain't got that swing.'"

"That's different."

"No, it ain't."

How pointless the arguments between us were. They went around and around and never solved anything, mainly because we both wanted to be right. I was right by sometimes admitting that I was wrong, but she has never admitted being at fault for anything, which made me even more right than her, right?

She filled a wine glass up to the rim from my boxed Chianti and it was only noon. "So, is Ted still with that teenager?" she asked.

"Yes, and they're both coming for dinner. Can you pour me a glass of that too?"

She poured me out a mug of Chianti.

"I liked his second wife, the one with the purple hair."

"That was the third one. The second one had that scorpion tattoo on her neck.

"All I know is that they all looked like they could've been his daughter." Bambi paused for a moment to take a big gulp of wine. "Think your dad would've traded me in for a newer model?"

"Yes. He would've put you out to pasture, saddle, and all."

We burst into unexpected laughter. It must have been the wine.

"Your dad wasn't one bit like Ted. Your dad acted his age. Ted never grew up. That's why he marries Barbie Dolls."

"I suppose they make him feel young. There's nothing wrong with that."

"I don't mind gettin' old, it's lookin' old that's a drag. But so far I've managed to keep all this in sexy workin' order." She made a sweeping gesture over her body, "Right?"

"Right."

There was a glint of vulnerability in her eyes that I'd never seen before. I felt an urge to hug her, but my stubborn pride held me back.

Much to my surprise Bambi gave me a tight hug. We held each other for a moment until I felt a sudden gush of tears. I felt embarrassed.

"Hey, what's goin' on?" Grace asked from the kitchen doorway. I didn't know how long she'd been standing there.

"We're just huggin' it out," said Bambi.

"Oh yeah? Cool. Can I go to Leslie's for dinner?"

"What? Are you serious?" I asked.

Bambi put her hands up and backed out of the kitchen. "I'm stayin' outta this one."

"I'm just asking that's all," said Gracie as if it wasn't a big deal.

"Why would you even ask?" I could barely contain my rage.

"Because Leslie asked me."

"Don't you want to be with your own family?"

"What family? It's just you, my loser uncle, and his retarded wife."

"She's not "retarded" and I've told you before to stop using that expression." Who was this monster that had taken over my daughter?

Gracie rolled her eyes as if she had heard this sermon once too often. "Whatever."

"No, this is not a 'whatever' this is important."

Gracie heaved a sigh as if I would never understand. "Forget it."

"So, you prefer Leslie's family to your own?"

"I said forget it."

I couldn't forget it. The last straw had been placed.

"If you want to go there for dinner, go there. I really don't care anymore where you go for Christmas." I could feel tears burning but I held them back. I hoped the "I-don't-care-any-more" really hurt her as much as she had just hurt me.

"Fine, I will then." She plugged in her earphones and left the kitchen, leaving me to deal with a fresh wave of tears.

When did Gracie change? Or is it I who have become less patient, less tolerant. She made me so angry. Did I resent her right from the start and I'm now just realizing it? Did I just have her out of a sense of duty?

I was going to give her up for adoption when she was born. There was a couple waiting, and all the papers were drawn up. I just couldn't go through with it. Once I saw her fighting little face, fresh out of the womb, I couldn't let her go.

I wondered if my mother thought about me that way. Even though she was high or drunk most of the time, I still felt she loved me. I tensed for a moment. Truth had a way of stabbing me at times. No, I never felt loved by her. That was a horrible thought. I pushed it from my mind.

"She gone?" Bambi asked returning to the kitchen.

I could only nod. Bambi hugged me again. "I think she just misses her grandpa as much as we do. She's just handlin' it differently."

Why didn't I think of that? Of course she missed her grampa. She was crazy about him and he doted on her. That's why she didn't want to be at home. But why couldn't she just have told me that?

CHAPTER 6

I'd finished setting the table with my good china, polished silverware, white linen, and hand-made centerpiece. It was just a crown of spruce twigs intertwined with red ribbons, centered with six red candles. There was one candle for each family member, including my dad. One candle refused to stand straight. Why was it that both our Christmas tree and this candle leaned to the left? It was just another small mystery to send out to the universe never to be solved.

The gray afternoon light filtered through the dining room windows. I wanted to light the candles right then and there. There has always been a magical glow in the moment just after candles are lit - a unique transcendence that invited harmony. It always made me feel hopeful for a closer bond between all who would be seated around my table. I lit all six candles, felt the magic, took a deep breath then blew them out. The enchantment dissolved.

I had ten minutes left to shower and change before Uncle Ted and Cindy arrived. I got halfway up the stairs when the doorbell rang. It wasn't like Uncle Ted to be early.

When I opened the front door, there was no one there. I stepped outside to see if anyone was around, but the street was vacant. I felt a shiver; was it my dad?

It wasn't like him to play tricks on me dead or alive. Still, I had to swallow back tears.

I stood in the opened doorway shivering and waiting for the mystery caller to reappear. I just couldn't bring myself to close the door. Out of the blue, I felt paralyzed with grief. Why this intensity so suddenly? I took in a deep breath and slowly let it out. I was able to move, but I wanted to be left alone with my grief. I wanted to leave, to run away. Is that what Joan did? She just ran away?

I grabbed my coat with the one pack of Camels left in its pocket. I was determined to quit after New Year. I stood on the porch and lit my cigarette. How comforting and seductive that smoke felt curling around my face. I managed to calm the urge to flee but I only had moments left before Uncle Ted arrived, and I was unwashed and still in my pajamas.

"Watcha doin' out here in the freezin' cold?" Bambi asked from behind me.

"Nothing. Just having a smoke." I turned to face her. She was wearing a hot pink mau-mau printed with large purple orchids and a straw hat festooned with plastic palm fronds.

"I know what you're thinkin'. What the hell am I wearin' this for, right?"

I took a drag from my cigarette rather than answer.

"It's to celebrate my honeymoon with your dad. 'Member, we went to Oahu and stayed at the Waikiki Biltmore and————"

"I'd better get ready. Uncle Ted's going to be here any minute." I moved past her and into the house. Hearing about their honeymoon was right up there with having my eye pierced with a hot needle.

* * *

Uncle Ted arrived an hour late, bearing an enormous gift basket wrapped in a silver ribbon emblazoned with "Compliments of The Bellagio." His bright red hair looked especially festive. "There's only so many of these baskets we can eat," he said handing me the basket. "So I thought you'd might enjoy one."

"The one we got from The Mirage was totally chocolate," said Cindy with a pout, "which I totally love, but now I can't eat anything for the next month."

"What about dinner?" I asked.

"I'm starting my diet tomorrow," she said giving me a hug.

"That's always been my motto," said Bambi sashaying past, muumuu flowing and drink in hand.

"You are rockin' that outfit," said Cindy. "It's totally not Christmas, which I totally get." Cindy was wearing a leopard print jumpsuit and stiletto gladiator heels.

I wanted to "totally" escape again, but I herded everyone into the living room.

Uncle Ted uncorked a bottle of red wine with an expensive-looking label. As usual, he started the conversation off with a story about his gambling escapades. This time it was about a high-stakes poker game where he won half a million dollars one night and lost it the next day. Bambi listened with that moth-to-a-flame look in her eyes. I feared her gambling addiction was reignited. "Money means nothing to me," said Uncle Ted as he reached over to dip a taco chip into a mound of salsa. That's when I noticed the ring, suitable for a cardinal, on the pinky finger of his right hand.

"That is so true, sweetie," said Cindy, leaning up against his shoulder like an adoring spaniel. "He's like so generous. I mean if he sees a single mother in the checkout line at Fry's, he buys her groceries every, single gosh-darn time."

"How does he know she's a single mother?" I asked.

"I've got a gambler's eye for detail. Nothing escapes me. Like, a few seconds ago you were looking at my ring, right?"

I blushed. "Well, it's hard to miss."

"I won it playing Texas Hold 'em with the Sultan of Malaysia."

"Oh, I used to play cards with him all the time," said Bambi filling her wine glass up to the rim. "Just me, him and the Queen of England."

"Wow," said Cindy with wide-eyed amazement. "I never knew she played Vegas."

"Oh, her and the Sultan hook up in Vegas all the time."

"Really?" asked Cindy.

"Sure, sweetie," answered Bambi.

Uncle Ted narrowed his eyes at Bambi, but she winked back.

"I haven't the faintest idea who the sultan-of-whatever is. But I'd still like to know how you can tell who's a single mother," I demanded.

"Well, obviously they have a kid with them," said Ted, "but the dead giveaway is that their hand shakes whenever they try to swipe a credit card." Both he and Cindy laughed.

"Well, I've been a single mom for fourteen years and my hand never shook swiping a credit card."

"That's because they were your dad's credit cards."

That was true, but he sounded so patronizing. It was time for me to check on the turkey before my anger took over.

Cindy followed me into the kitchen. "Can I help with anything?"

I began basting the turkey. "Thanks, but I think I've got everything under control."

"My mom never cooked nuthin," she said opening one of my cupboards. "We had frozen dinners or McDonald's every day," she scanned the contents of the shelves. "But I'm gonna learn to cook someday, just as soon as my career gets goin.'" She closed the cupboard door. "I love your cupboards, they're so nice and cluttered."

I wasn't sure how to take this comment so I plunged past it. "How's your career going?"

"Nowhere fast. I'm gettin' real sick of Vegas. Most of the people I meet there are totally wasted and only lookin' for an extremely good time, know what I mean? I mean like one guy said he'd give me a thousand bucks for a blowjob. Can you believe that? I mean I get depressed a lot. I mean like all the time. Is there any more wine?"

She looked a lot more fragile than I'd ever noticed before.

"Sure, help yourself." I pointed to my box of Chianti.

"Hey, is this where the party is?" asked Bambi swaying into the room spilling some of her wine onto her mau mau.

"I was just checking the turkey. We're going to eat soon."

Bambi downed the remains of her wine, "We should all be singin' carols or somethin.'"

"Yeah, that would be fun!" said Cindy clapping excitedly.

Bambi started singing way off key, "Good King Washin'slosh looked out, on the feast of somethin'…somethin…'"

"No, it's Good King Wishin'-less…" said Cindy.

I wondered if these two ladies would still be upright by dinner or, more importantly, would I?

Bambi suddenly burst into tears. "That was your dad's favorite Christmas carol."

I'd never seen Bambi cry before. I wasn't sure what to do, especially when I was still holding the turkey baster. Cindy put her arms around Bambi.

"Aww sweetie, don't cry. My cat Louie died on Christmas, so I'm kind I've feelin' the same thing."

"I'm not talkin' 'bout a friggin' cat!" said Bambi pushing her away.

Cindy's face tightened into such a wounded look; it made me look away.

"What's goin' on in here?" asked Uncle Ted coming into the kitchen.

Cindy pointed at Bambi, "It's her – she doesn't care that Louie died on Christmas."

Bambi, now apparently unsure of what she'd done, blinked back at Cindy.

Cindy started sobbing and pushed her head against Uncle Ted's chest.

Bambi grabbed my box of Chianti and staggered out of the kitchen. "Merry Fuckin' Christmas."

"I warned your dad about marrying her," said Uncle Ted after Bambi was safely out of hearing range. "She never had any filter on what she said or cared about who she hurt. She almost cost him this house. Your dad was always picking up damaged women, thinking he could fix them, but he never could."

"And isn't that what you do too? Pick up young women and try to "fix" them by buying them bigger boobs?" I said and immediately regretted it.

"My boobs aren't fixed." Cindy insisted through her tears. "They're as real as apple pie."

"Cindy just wanted her nose done, so I..."

"No, I didn't. That's what you wanted!" Cindy's tears stop. She was now furious. She pushed Uncle Ted away.

"No, honey. You asked me———"

"What was wrong with my old nose?"

"Nothing was wrong with it but you———"

"You just hate me for who I am! Cindy sounded more now like a child having a tantrum. "I'm leaving!" She turned and marched out of the kitchen.

Uncle Ted turned to me. "Well, I hope you're satisfied.

"What do you mean?"

"You know exactly what I mean. Regardless of what you think of me, your dad was always very proud of you. But I don't think he'd be too proud of you right now."

Within minutes, I was alone in the kitchen with a twenty-five-pound cooked turkey, all the trimmings, and, of course, the leftover mess of yet another family get- together disaster.

There was only one thing left for me to do. The one thing I had done all my life when everything around me collapsed. I slid down to the floor, hugged my knees to my chest and rocked myself back and forth until I felt safe again. I'm not sure how long I sat like this, but when I was ready I stood up and headed into the dining room.

I was hoping to recapture the moment when I first lit the candles. Just as I was about to light them, a voice came from behind me.

"Where's everyone?" I turned to see Gracie standing behind me.

"They all left." I gave her a fierce hug. "I'm so glad you're here. How was your dinner?"

"I didn't stay. They're nice, but I'd rather have crazy. So, why'd everyone leave?"

"Too much wine and anger. You know, the usual. You must be hungry."

"Yeah."

"Well, then, let's eat."

I brought out the turkey and all the trimmings and Gracie and I ate, laughed, and talked with ease for the first time in a very long time

There's always some magical harmony in the air around Christmas.

CHAPTER 7

I've had my job at the Quick Trip for over five years. Before that, I cleaned houses until Gracie's embarrassment forced me to quit. She discovered I was her friend's mom's cleaning lady.

I planned to go back to school to get my G.E.D. so I could get a more fulfilling, or better-paying job, but so far it's been easier to float along in my low-demanding and very low-paying job.

Imogene, my co-worker, says I'm afraid to dream big. Her big dream is to become a lawyer for the "down and outers." She quit school after Grade Eight, has worked at the Quick Trip for fifteen years, and is 48 years old. Good luck getting into law school. But who am I to step on someone's dream. At least she has one.

Like me, she got pregnant when she was a teenager, but unlike me, Imogene's family told her she was "on the express lane to hell" and they would not welcome any "bastard" child. They forced her to give her baby up for adoption.

Imogene's the only friend I have, but I wish, snob that I am, she was a little more refined. She drops her "g's", swears a lot, weighs over 200 pounds, cracks her gum, wears far too much fluorescent blue eye shadow, and doesn't care if her brown roots show through her bleached blond hair. She says letting your roots show is "real in" now and she started the trend.

I'm very proud of my vocabulary, but when I use simpler words with her, she comes at me with "Don't talk down to me like that. I'm not a dummy. Someday I'll be practicin' law."

I wish Imogene were more like Joan: educated, sophisticated, and cool. I wish I were too.

There is nothing remotely cool or sophisticated about working at the Quick Trip.

Walter, the store manager, is ten years younger than me but acts twenty years older. He wears a shirt protector for his pens and his favorite song is Wayne Newton's *"Danke Shoen,"* which he whistles constantly until you're ready to scream. He tries his best to assert his authority over Imogene and me, but we counter by making lewd hand gestures behind his back.

Walter insists that the "customer is always right." He's come very close to firing me because I've broken that rule on a few occasions. But not having a job would be very bad for my budget, so, I've swallowed my anger and kept my smile frozen.

However, yesterday all bets were off. Yesterday I felt like a scorpion ready to strike.

I was dealing with one of my Grade A pain-in-the-ass customers. The name on her credit card, believe it or not, was "B. Hitch." I could always tell when she entered the store because her perfume marched ahead of her like a nuclear cloud. Her face was cemented in place by one too many Botox injections making her look recently embalmed.

For some reason, she always picked my register and always had some "helpful" but cutting remark like, "I know a good conditioner for that hair of yours," or "Are you aware there are some deodorants that work better than others?"

Generally, I just bite my tongue and hold back the urge to stab her hand with my pen.

She was checking out a whole cartload of "No Gain" a no-carb, no-taste pudding. To protect her recently manicured nails, which were blood-red and claw-like, she took each can out of the basket with excruciating care. The whole process took about a minute a can.

She stopped to give me the once over.

"Put on a little weight over Christmas, I see. You'd better watch that. A woman like you can't afford to gain any more weight."

I took a deep breath, but it didn't help. "Could you pick up those cans a little faster?" I said trying to keep a level tone. "You're holding up the line." There was only one woman behind her.

She took in a sharp breath and looked at me like I was a cockroach. "No store clerk, like you, will dictate to me how I empty my cart."

"What do you mean *like me*?" All my blood had rushed to my head and it was about to explode.

"Well, it's obvious."

"What's *obvious*?"

"Why don't you just be quiet and do your job."

Something bad snapped in my brain. "Why don't you go fuck yourself."

The lady behind her gasped but then gave me a thumbs- up. I felt as triumphant as "Norma Rae". But the glory was short-lived.

Ms. Hitch yelled for Walter. Walter confronted me and demanded I apologize. I refused. In fact, I told Walter to fuck off too. He fired me on the spot.

Ms. Hitch was victorious, and I was jobless.

On the drive home, the consequence of my rebellion slapped me in the face like a wet towel. I had $75.86 left in my bank account, and all my credit cards were maxed out, thanks to Christmas.

Uncle Ted immediately came to mind. I could borrow money from him, but that would mean I'd have to apologize for the Christmas fiasco. I'd rather starve than swallow my pride, but that would mean Gracie and Bambi would starve too. Bambi had a small pension but not enough to keep us all afloat. In fact, I've been supporting both of them since my dad died.

My cell phone went off. It was Imogene. It suddenly occurred to me that I was angry with B. Hitch because she looked down on me exactly the way I looked down on Imogene.

I pulled over to answer the cell.

"What happened?" asked Imogene.

"I got fired."

"You told Walter to fuck off?"

"Yes, but first I told B. Hitch to do that."

"Well, fuck me right up the ass – I wish I'd been there to see it."

"Yeah, well, it got me canned."

"He can't just fire you like that. There's gotta be a law about it."

"He warned me many, many times."

"Then, fuck him and Quick Trip. Just fuck 'em all right up their Quick Trip ass. That's all I can say. Maybe I'll quit, too, outta protest. "

"No! Don't do that. You've got rent to pay. At least I don't have to worry about that."

"So what're ya gonna do?"

"I don't know." A big wave of tears hit me.

"Okay, okay. Where are you?"

"I just pulled off the highway."

"Meet me at The Blue and we'll get shit-faced - my treat."

"Thanks, but I really don't feel like it."

"What? Since when have you not felt like gettin' wasted?"

"Maybe later. Just not now. I need some time by myself."

"Well, don't take too much time. Call me, okay?"

"I will."

Her voice softened, "You need a break, girlfriend."

"I'm sure I'm in for a real long break."

I drove back onto the highway but had no idea where I was headed. For ten years my daily routine had an unchanging purpose, but now I was aimless. It was scary. I couldn't just drive without a destination; it cost too much gas.

What had I done? How would I get another job? I had no training in anything.

I was such a loser. I didn't care anymore. The urge to run away had come back - just the open road and me. It sounded wonderful. Bambi would look after Gracie. It was painfully apparent that Gracie was closer to her than me. *They will both do fine without me.*

If only my dad was with me. He'd take of everything. It hit me how much I had depended on him. I was even driving his old car: a 1990 Infinity that needed an oil change.

Perhaps I never grew up. Perhaps I was more like my mom than I thought. What was it that made me still miss her so much? She died over ten years ago, without ever seeing Gracie or me again. My dad knew how she died but I told him I didn't want to know. I had a pretty good idea how and I didn't need a detailed description.

Joan's disappearance didn't seem so mysterious after all. Maybe she just got tired of her life too and wanted to start a new one. Can you start a new life without running away from your old one?

That night I found myself out on my porch, way past midnight, smoking one cigarette after another from a pack I stole from the Quick Trip as a going-away present. Each worry multiplied and quadrupled. Would I ever find another job? I had to slash my budget even closer to the bone, no more cable, no more Hagen Daz, no more cigarettes.

I immediately grabbed another cigarette and lit it from the one I was already smoking.

"Hey, what's eatin' you?"

I jumped from my seat. Bambi was standing next to me.

"Sorry, I didn't mean to scare you."

"That's okay," I said without really meaning it. I just wanted to be alone. "I've just got a lot on my mind."

"I knew that the minute you got home today. Plus Imogene told me you got fired. Why didn't *you* tell me?"

I was immediately furious with Imogene. She had no right to do that. She had no boundaries, no sense of discretion.

"And don't be mad at Imogene, be mad at me 'cause I promised her I wouldn't tell you, but when you didn't tell me I kind of couldn't hold it back. But if you ask me, it's 'bout time you quit that friggin' job. You got way more goin' for you than workin' at the Quick Trip."

I had heard this before from Bambi, and instead of making me feel better, it made me feel worse. I was just too lazy to better myself, or maybe I was just too afraid. *Afraid of what?*

"Yes, you're right. I'm sure there's something better for me out there. I'm sure it will come along."

"I don't buy that little memorized speech of yours and neither do you. I've been watchin' you for the past few months you've been really mopin' around here more so than usual. You gotta let yer dad go and stand on your own"

Now she was making me angry. How dare she lecture me on how to live – she was a gambling addict. I took a few sharp drags on the remains of my cigarette.

"I miss him too but he wouldn't want us to stop livin' and enjoyin' ourselves, betterin' ourselves."

I wondered when she was going to start bettering herself. I was getting angry enough to ask that, but something held me back. Tolerance? No, I was just worn out. I just wanted to be by myself. I stubbed out my cigarette and stood up. "I'm going to bed."

CHAPTER 8

It's been a week since I've been fired and I still haven't gotten out of my pajamas. I also had not checked the mail for Eric as I had promised. I put on an overcoat and headed over to this place.

His mailbox was overflowing. Some of it had fallen to the porch and had been water-stained by recent snowfalls.

I picked up all the mail and unlocked his front door.

There is a line from a poem by Dorothy Parker that sums up my life.

"Four be the things I'd been better without,

Love, curiosity, freckles, and doubt."

I can live with freckles, but the other three, especially curiosity, have only brought cats and me trouble. On my eighth birthday, I jumped off a tree branch fifteen feet above ground to see if I could fly. I broke both ankles finding out. A year later, I was curious about breathing underwater and almost drowned.

As I grew older, I handled my curiosity with more maturity and intelligence. Oh really? Then why am I standing in Eric's vestibule, having put his two-weeks of mail on a hall table and now thinking about going for a private tour of the house?

Because I have no control over my curiosity, once it's ignited there's no putting it out.

I head down a hallway until I reach the living room - which is like walking into an igloo. The walls, furniture, and carpet are all white. The only sparks of color come from a few photographs, all of which are of Eric and Angela. There is none of Joan. I feel a shiver, like something very cold wafted by. Perhaps that's Joan's spirit trying to send me a message.

I go into the kitchen, which looks space-age modern and clean enough for surgery. There's a stainless-steel work island in the center that reminds me of an autopsy table. Glass doors screen the cupboards. All the china is lined up in rigid symmetry. Even the canned goods and boxed food are arranged this way, according to size, shape, and color.

Except for the autopsy table, I want to have a life that has a kitchen like this. My cupboards are arranged according to the rules of random chaos. No wonder I'm never calm. Do I attract turmoil? Am I addicted to it? Yes. That's why I'm trespassing through someone's home.

I climb the stairs to the bedrooms.

The master bedroom has all the trimmings of an upscale bordello. There's a ceiling mirror over the bed, which has red satin sheets and heart-shaped pillows. In the center of the room is a stripper pole. Wow. I cannot imagine Joan on a stripper pole, but I think Angela could handle one.

I don't think I've ever had a sexual experience like the sex Eric and Angela must have in here. It's all been very conventional, and infrequent. In fact, the last time I had sex was over a year ago - no, it was more like three years to be honest. It was in the backseat of a car of one of my internet dates. He introduced me to my first tequila shot, and many more after that. What followed is just a blurry memory. I don't even remember his name and I'm sure he doesn't remember mine. It makes me very sad.

How pathetic I am invading Eric and Angela's privacy but that doesn't stop me from checking the nightstand. I'm not surprised by the fur-covered handcuffs and some kind of whip-like thing, but the Bible?

Just then I hear a noise from downstairs. Someone is entering the house. I hear Eric's voice. "Looks like Alice collected the mail."

Why are they here? They're supposed to return next week!

I can't move. Maybe this is just a nightmare and I'm going to wake up soon. No, it's actually happening. Electrified panic sets in. I look over at the bedroom window. I could jump out of it, but that's a good twenty-foot drop. I could hide in the closet. No, that won't work. The closet is the first thing they'll open. I hear them coming up the stairs. I can't breathe. I'm going to faint.

I have to do something. I just can't stand here. I look over at the bed, there just might be enough room for me to fit under it. I squeeze under the bed just in time before Eric comes into the room.

"Did you leave the side table drawer open?" asks Eric.

"No, I didn't. Someone's been up here," says Angela.

"You're just being paranoid. No one's been here."

"Yes, they have. I just know they have."

I can feel sweat running down the side of my face. I hold my breath afraid they might hear me breathing.

Dear God, don't let them find me and I promise I will never do this again.

"Maybe it was Alice," said Eric.

I feel woozy. I might vomit. I deserve this. I'm going to crawl out from under this bed and reveal myself. That would be the right thing to do, but I don't.

"Or maybe it was Joan. Maybe she came back" said Angela.

"No, that's impossible," said Eric.

"What do you mean, that's impossible?"

I can't hear Eric's answer, but I sure would like to. *Why would it be "impossible?*

They leave the room. I can still hear their voices but not what they're saying. I hear the downstairs door close. Have they both left the house? If they have I can't lose this opportunity to escape. I've never felt such a rush of relief in my life.

I make a mad dash for the stairwell. My foot slips off the first tread and I bounce down the steps on my rear. Thank God the stairs are carpeted but I may no longer have a backbone, not that I ever had one.

I race to the back door, but when I open it an alarm goes off. I run out closing it behind me. In a remarkable leap, I manage to vault over the fence, but I land hard on my cement patio. I feel a stab of pain in one ankle. I think I may have broken or sprained it. Somehow I manage to make it to my back door and enter my house just in time to hear our front door bell ring. My ankle is throbbing but I can still walk on it, so it must not be broken.

It suddenly occurs to me that I still have their key.

I hear Bambi yell from upstairs "Will somebody get the friggin' door!"

I have just enough time to grab a tea towel to wipe the sweat off my forehead and hobble to the front door.

CHAPTER 9

I put on my best-surprised face when I opened my front door. "Oh you're back already! Come in."

Eric looked tense but his tone was even. "Yeah, Angela came down with the flu, and the weather was bad, so we left early. Listen, have you been in our house at all?"

"Just to drop off the mail like you asked me."

"When was that?"

"Oh, just sometime this morning."

"Because our backdoor alarm just went off."

"Were you in the house when we came home?" asked Angela glaring at me.

"No, of course not," I said. I could tell she knew I was lying.

Eric nudged her to calm down, but she didn't back down.

"Do you still have the key?" asked Eric.

"Yes, of course," I dug into my pocket and handed him the key, but my hand was shaking. He saw this, and so did Angela.

"Is there something wrong with your ankle?" asked Angela.

I put my injured foot down and tried not to wince. "No, it's fine." I could feel sweat on my forehead.

"We believe someone was in our home, and they may have still been there when we came home," said Eric.

"Oh my God. That's terrible," I answered. I hated liars and hypocrites but I was becoming a charter member of their club.

"Did you see anyone?" asked Eric.

"No, I've been home all morning and I haven't seen anyone. But you should call the police and report this."

"Yes, we intend to do that," said Angela. There was a little less harshness in her voice but she still seemed wary. I find that women can "read" people way better than men.

"Well, thanks for putting the mail away, and sorry to bother you," said Eric.

"Oh, it's no bother at all." I said, incredibly relieved they were backing away. I thought about asking them about their trip, but my ankle was throbbing and I wasn't sure how much longer I could keep up my bullshit.

Eric headed out the door but Angela stayed behind and gave me a coy smile.

"There seems to be something stuck on your shoe," she said.

I looked down to see a horrifying sight. It appeared to be the end of a used condom sticking out from under my shoe. It must have adhered itself to my shoe when I was hiding under their bed. This was a moment where one hopes the earth opens up and swallows them. I could feel my face reddening. Words failed me.

"That's okay I understand," said Angela softly in my ear and gave me a wink before heading out the door.

CHAPTER 10

For the first time in my life, I was on unemployment insurance. I had sent out 100 resumes going from the top jobs that I was qualified for, which narrowed the field considerably, and working my way down to the bottom (cleaning public bathrooms), but heard nothing back from any of them. I wasn't surprised, the country was in a recession and everyone was looking for a job.

I went through the motions of putting myself out there but most days I just drove to the park where I used to take Gracie when she was little. I carried her in a baby sling on the hiking trails, and then when she was able to walk on her own we walked together. Walking with a child in Nature is like rediscovering everything. She would pick up a twig and examine it like it was a Masterpiece, which in fact reminded me that it was.

But now I didn't even hike the trails. I just sat in my car smoking one cigarette after another.

I wanted my crappy job back. At least it provided me with a steady income. Tomorrow I would swallow my pride and call Walter. I would apologize to him and even to B. Hitch. My big mouth and I deserved that humiliation.

I thought about my run-in with Eric and Angela, and my stuck-on safe. I'm sure Angela thought I was a hooker, but that was easier to deal with than her knowing the truth about that safe.

I was just about to light up another smoke, when Joan appeared at the driver's window. My mouth opened in shock and the cigarette fell into my lap.

I'm not sure how long I stared at her through the closed window. I wanted to make sure I wasn't seeing another apparition. She looked like she hadn't slept in weeks. Her eyes were red-rimmed and bloodshot

I just couldn't keep staring at her but I had to fight the urge to press the window button. She looked like she was capable of anything.

She spoke softly. "Sorry, I didn't mean to scare you."

"Joan, is that really you?"

"Yes, it's me all right."

"Where have you been?"

"I've been on the road mostly but I came back just before Christmas."

"Was that you at Wal-Mart?"

"Yes, and that was me ringing your doorbell Christmas Eve."

"Why?"

"I don't know. I don't know what happened to me but I'm trying to come back. I've been watching your house and following you. I guess that sounds pretty creepy, right?"

"Right."

"Ever since that night we had that talk, I've felt a sense of connection with you. I'm sorry we didn't get to know each other better, before it all happened."

"Before what happened?"

"I really can't talk here. I might be seen. I have to go now. Please don't tell Eric you saw me."

"Where are you going?"

She started moving away from me towards the woods. There was no other car parked in the lot. So she must have come on foot.

I yelled after "Why can't I tell Eric?"

"He threatened to kill me!" she yelled back then turned and ran into the woods.

CHAPTER 11

It was the first time, I'd seen the inside of the Washte police station. It wasn't like the small-town Mayberry Sherriff's setup seen on 70's T.V. There was a glass partition sealing off the office from direct contact with any visitors.

Sherriff Carton approached the glass partition. He didn't seem to remember me from our last interview about Joan. He greeted me with a cool "Good morning, ma'am. What can I do for you?"

"I'm here about my missing neighbor, Joan Lewis." His face remained inscrutable.

"You interviewed me about her a few months back."

He just nodded. Why did it bother me so much that he didn't remember me?

"You're Alice Birdwhistle?" he added.

His answer startled me for a moment. Another misjudgment on my part.

"Yes."

"What information do you have about Joan?"

I was still recovering from him remembering my name, and what was even worse I was blushing. "Well, she's no longer missing. I saw her in the park today." In a stuttering and stammering manner that I tried very hard to keep smooth, I went on to describe my meeting with Joan in every detail I could remember. He wrote everything I said down on a notepad, never once inviting me to come into the office and sit down where we would both be more comfortable.

"Did she say she would contact you again?"

"No, she just took off."

He raised his eyebrows. "I'll have to report this to her husband?"

Dreading what was soon to be another meeting with Eric, I just nodded.

"Would you read this over please," he continued, "Just to make sure I've written down the information you gave me correctly and if I have, just sign it on the bottom." He slid the paper he had written down my information through an opening in the glass partition, that's when I noticed he wasn't wearing a wedding band.

While I read over his notes, I could feel his eyes on me. I glanced up at him a few times, trying to look just a bit alluring but his expression remained blank. Why was I always interested in men that weren't really interested in me?

"Yes, you got everything right," I said sliding the paper back through the partition. "Is there anything else?" I said, putting a sharp tone to my voice, just to show him that it didn't matter to me that he wasn't reacting to my "charms".

"No, thanks. That's all." And with that, he picked up the board and walked back to his desk.

What a complete asshole. Hell hath no fury like a woman scorned.

CHAPTER 12

The Blue Moon Café is a little oasis of diversity within a 500-mile radius of conformity. It's on Whakan Street, which is supposed to be the Lakota word for a shooting star. It was named after the founder's wife.

Whakan Street was once the heart and soul of Washte's business district which included: Norman's Groceries, Marley's Fashions, Lena's Jewelry and Hair Salon, Mason's Hardware and Tractor Repair, and Hope's Pharmacy. It can be walked from end to end in just over twenty minutes. These stores had been in Washte for generations, but they're all boarded up and abandoned now. Walmart can be thanked for that. One was built just outside of town two years ago. Lured by lower prices, we Washteans migrated to Wal-Mart even though we felt ashamed for doing so.

Nevertheless, two operations that survived the Walmart invasion: the Washte Credit Union, The Quick Trip, and "The Blue Moon Café".

Marlene Dover owns and runs the "Blue". She's a large shapely woman, with a round face and luminous blue eyes. Her thick white hair has a blue streak running through it and is held up with Geisha hair combs which is not something normally worn by the women of Washte. It looks both exotic and ageless.

Marlene's managed to create a common ground at her Cafe that draws a diverse crowd from grim-faced farmers to tattooed, nose-ringed millennials. For the late-night crowd, Marlene sets up a bar, clears some space for a dance floor, and turns on the jukebox, circa 1960, where customers can hear everything from "Chain of Fools" to "I Fall to Pieces."

The Blue stays open as long as there are bodies drinking or dancing. Marlene's last-call ritual is playing "Blue Moon" on her ukulele. Everyone sings along.

I know nothing about Marlene's past, but I believe it's marked with a lot of love gone wrong, something I can definitely relate to. Her menu features items like "I Miss You Macaroni", "Where You Bean Salad" and "Heartbreak Hamburger."

She's furnished the "Blue" with Parisian-style wicker chairs and tables, about ten of them all total. She claims they are exact replicas of the chairs used at the *Les Deux Magots* a café in Paris, where Hemingway and Picasso hung out. In fact one of the tables, she claims, was sat at by Hemingway, but she won't tell which one.

There's a twenty-foot-long black arborite counter with red vinyl seats atop silver stands. On the wall behind it is a pass-through window to the kitchen. Seven dark mahogany booths are linked together below a picture window. The booths can seat six people if half of them are kids. The picture window runs the length of the room affording a panoramic view of Whakan Street. A fluorescent neon tube, positioned in the middle of the window, spells out "*The Blue Moon Café*" in flickering blue letters.

The room is painted in serviceable white but taped to the walls are a series of old film noir movie posters. My favorites are *The Maltese Falcon*, *Double Indemnity*, and *Laura*. Next to the entrance door is a bulletin board where people can post anything they want. Currently, there is a birth announcement, an obituary, a yard sale, helpful household hints, a potato salad recipe, a picture of a missing dog which looks suspiciously like a coyote, and Joan, my no-longer-missing neighbor.

There is another service Marlene offers for some of us Washteans. She is someone to go to and talk about problems that you don't feel comfortable sharing with anyone else – a Washtean therapist.

She's just poured me a fresh cup of coffee. "You did the right thing, going to the police. But if she doesn't feel safe about doing that herself, she can hide away until she does. Meanwhile the Sheriff doesn't have to search for her anymore."

"He's a real cool character, isn't he."

"He's been through a lot"

"He has? Like what?

"He comes in here for coffee and a bagel to take out every morning. He's polite but seldom smiles. I'm pretty sure he's ex-military, so he was probably in Iraq or Afghanistan, but I thought you wanted to talk about Joan." She said with a wink, and that wink meant she was picking up something from me, and that "something" was something I really didn't want to get into.

I took a sip of my coffee to collect myself. "I just don't understand what Joan's trying to do. Why run away from everything and just come back and tell me about it? I don't even know her. I mean what is her plan? What does she hope to achieve?"

"She's scared. Haven't you ever just wanted to run away?"

It's amazing how Marlene could ask just the right question without putting you down. She was so right this time. "Yes. Haven't you?"

"Oh, I've ran away many times, but no matter how far you run to, you can't run away from yourself."

"What did you run away from?"

"Someday I'll tell you about it but I can't now. The lunch crowd should be here pretty soon. Time to put some Heartbreak Hamburgers on the grill."

So Marlene's past will remain a mystery – another one to add to the goings-on in Washte. I guess we're all a bit mysterious. Even parts of me remain a mystery to myself.

CHAPTER 13

That next morning I got a call from Eric. Sheriff Carton hadn't wasted any time telling him about my run in with Joan.

"Why didn't you call me first?" he yelled through the phone receiver.

"Because I ————"

"Or at least let me know after you talked with the Sherriff___"

"Because I wasn't sure___"

"I mean after all, Alice, we've been neighbors for over ten years. The decent thing to do would have been to let me know first. Right?"

"Well, I thought about it and___"

"You thought about it? Why didn't you just do it?"

Something snapped inside me, like it did at the Quick Pick. "Why don't you just go fuck yourself." I pressed the "end call" button on my cell phone. Of course, within seconds my phone buzzed again. I let it go to voice mail and shut off the ringer on my phone.

I now could see what Joan was afraid of. I'd never heard this side of Eric before. But after a few moments, I reconsidered this. He had everything right to be angry. I mean after all, he had been held under suspicion for all these months, but I still didn't like him.

"Who was that?" asked Gracie coming into the kitchen.

"Eric. I just hung up on him."

"You did?" she asked with a conspiratorial smile.

"Because I saw his wife yesterday."

Gracie's eyes widened even larger. "You did?"

"Yes, and she was worried Eric was___

Just then the doorbell rang. I was pretty certain who the caller was.

"Going to kill her?" asked Grace.

I nodded and the doorbell rang again.

"Don't answer it," Gracie moved in front of me. "Maybe he's got a gun, or a knife or___"

I put my hands on her shoulders. "I'm not going to let him intimidate me, but I'll check through the side window."

I looked through the side window to see if Eric wasn't carrying anything lethal. He was just standing there without anything in his hands and his head down.

"I'm gonna get my baseball bat," Gracie whispered from behind me.

"No, you're not. If you're that afraid, go into the kitchen and stand by the phone, okay?"

"Okay."

I waited for her to go back to the kitchen, then I took in a deep breath and opened the door.

Eric stood before me bleary-eyed, and unshaven, "I'm sorry" he said sounding very genuine. "Sheriff Carton dropped by late last night and told me you'd seen Joan and that she'd accused me of trying to kill her, which is totally untrue."

Now I wasn't sure who to believe. "Would you like to come in?" I said hoping he didn't want to come in.

"I can't right now. I'm already late for work."

Gracie appeared next to me at the door.

"She's getting quite grown up," he said, smiling at Grace.

What a strange thing for him to say at this moment and something in his tone made me cringe. I was back to believing Joan.

"Fuck you, asshole," said Gracie turning around and heading back into the kitchen. I felt like I should reprimand her but I didn't.

"I guess she took me the wrong way," he said with a little smirk.

"Yes, she did." I said as flatly as I could. I felt such a sudden wave of rage swell up. I wanted to slap that smirk off his face. I don't know how Joan had put up with him for so long.

"Listen you don't know how it feels to be under suspicion for six months that you've killed your wife. You have no idea."

"No, I don't."

"And I just wish you had told me you'd seen her. Are you going to see her again?"

"No, she just left without giving me her number or address or anything."

"If you see her again, will you please tell her to contact me?"

"I will."

I just want you and I to be friends."

I swallowed an uncomfortable gulp.

He reached out to shake my hand. Friendship was the last thing I wanted from him but nevertheless, I reached across, and we shook hands. "I'd still like to talk with you," he insisted. "Would you like to get together for a coffee or something?

Was the coming on to me?

"I mean with Angela and I." He must have read my thoughts.

I could feel sweat beads forming on my forehead. "Sure, but I've been so busy, you know, looking for a job and all."

"Yeah, it's rough out there, but could you just spare a little time?"

Shit. There was no way I could avoid meeting with them. "Okay."

We made arrangements to meet for coffee at the Blue.

CHAPTER 14

The next morning, Bambi came into the kitchen just as I was finishing my one too many coffees. Usually, she wore shapeless housedresses and no makeup. This morning she was wearing a tiger-stripe top, which could barely contain her ample bosom, front and sides, black spandex pants, silver stiletto heels, and was fully made up including fluttering false eyelashes and scarlet red lipstick.

"Are you just getting in?" I asked, afraid of the answer.

"Yeah, I was doin' a little business." She plunked a large zebra-striped bag on the kitchen table. "And it was the best time I've had in a long time."

"Doing what?"

"As soon as you get that stick out of your ass, I'll tell you."

I looked over at the zebra-striped bag. Gracie breezed in with her head bopping in time to whatever was playing on her plugged-in iPhone. She stopped when she saw Bambi.

"O-M-G you are rockin' that outfit."

"Thanks, sweetie," said Bambi and nudged Gracie while she pointed to the bag.

Gracie pulled out her earplugs. "What's in that?"

"Why don't you go see?"

Gracie's eyes lit up like she'd won the lottery. She grabbed the bag, unzipped the top, and pulled out a wad of freshly-minted hundred-dollar bills wrapped in a currency strap. "Holy Shit."

"There's about fifty more of 'em in there," said Bambi turning to me. "My little contribution to the keepin'-our-heads-above water fund. I found a hot game last night, put down my pension cheque and played all night riding my winnin' streak til dawn."

"Unfriggin' believable," said Gracie digging through the rest of the cash-filled bag.

Gracie's adoration for Bambi had now reached new limits but I was about to put a big wet blanket over it all. And I believed I deserved the Nobel Prize for "I think I'm doing the Right Thing."

"Mom, say something. I mean Bambi just saved our asses."

And, of course, now my daughter's language was coming out of the toilet, but then so was mine.

"Gracie, I want to talk to Bambi privately."

"Why privately?" Gracie demanded. "Why can't I hear it? Aren't I a part of this family too?"

Bambi put her arm around Gracie like they were a united front. "You can say whatever ya wanna say in front of her. It's okay with me."

I'm not sure what was motivating me, but I hated Bambi more than ever.

"I cannot accept this money, Bambi."

"What?" Gracie stared at me wide-eyed with disbelief.

I took a deep breath and continued. "You promised me that you'd never go back to gambling. If I accept this money, then I'd be a co-dependent. I'd be condoning___"

"Mom, that is just so crazy___"

"Gracie, if you're going to stay here. Don't interrupt me."

"But she's just trying to help!"

"Gracie put the money back in the bag."

"I'm not givin' that to you," Bambi countered. "I'm givin' it to Gracie."

Gracie glared at me defiantly.

"Don't do this to me, Bambi. She is my daughter and I will not allow her to accept___

Gracie threw the money at me. "You're such a bitch!" and stormed out of the kitchen.

"There you go, Miss High and Mighty," said Bambi. "I hope you're satisfied. I'll be findin' myself another place to live, and you can stay here by your lonely-old-holier-than-thou self."

Bambi picked up the zebra bag and marched out.

I looked down at the wad of bills Gracie threw at me. I wasn't even sure how I was going to buy food. Sometimes doing the "right" thing is way more complicated than it should be. I bent down and picked up the bills.

CHAPTER 15

A gray squirrel, wearing a black Stetson, was perched on my bedpost. He announced, in the voice of Steven Colbert, that I'd won a billion dollars and had ten minutes to claim my prize. I jumped out of bed but couldn't move. My feet were glued to the floor. I was also completely naked. I managed to yank my duvet off the bed and wrapped it around myself.

The Squirrel was now at my feet, looking up at me, "Five minutes and counting!"

While I struggled to pull my feet up, someone else was pulling on my duvet. "Hurry up. Hurry up!"

"I can't! I'm stuck!"

I woke up to see Gracie standing over my bed pulling on my duvet. "Wake up! She's gone! She's gone!"

"Who's gone?"

"Bambi! She left this." She handed me a note.

The note read: "Take good care of yourself, baby girl. And don't forget how much I love you."

Gracie collapsed in tears on my bed. She looked so small and vulnerable. It took me back to when she was a baby when I could comfort her just by rocking her in my arms. She wouldn't let me do that anymore.

"I'm sure she's not gone for good," I said.

"It's all your fault she left."

"Yes, I guess, it is. I'm sorry."

Gracie blinked back at me a bit surprised because I rarely admitted when I had made a mistake. I feared if I didn't she wouldn't trust me.

Gracie wiped her eyes with the back of her sleeve. "You were too hard on her. She was just trying to help."

"Yeah, you're right. I thought I was doing the right thing."

She paused for a moment, "I mean I know she's like an addict but not like a junkie."

An alarm bell went off in my head. Junkie? Where had she learned that term?"

"There's a girl in my class who's a junkie," she continued matter-of-factly. "I thought that drugs were the only kind of addiction but then this man came to our class and told us there're lots of types."

I wasn't sure whether to ask her if they sold drugs in her school, or had she been approached to buy drugs. I decided this wasn't the best time to question her about drugs.

"Like if you can't help but gamble away everything, that's an addiction too," she continued. "But it's not like Bambi won that money for herself. She was just trying to help us, right?"

"Yes, I think she was."

Gracie acquiesced with a sigh. "What's going to happen to her?"

"I don't know."

"Is she gonna end up alone in some awful place?"

"I hope not."

"You're not going to take off too, are you?"

Her question startled me for a second. I felt a stab of tears, but I swallowed them down. "Why would you even think that?"

"I dunno. You're just so angry with me all the time."

"Just because I get angry with you, doesn't mean I'd leave you. I'll always be there for you. Got that?"

She wiped her nose again with her sleeve and nodded.

"Is that a yes?

"Yes."

"Okay. I'm sorry if I've been overreacting a bit lately, but I'm under a lot of pressure what with losing my job.

"I might have a job soon. This lady asked me to babysit her kids for a few hours a week. So I can bring in a little money.

I gave her a tight hug and she didn't resist. "You know something. You are an exceptional young lady. I don't tell you that enough, do I."

Gracie shrugged with an embarrassed grin.

"We'll both get through this together." I reached my hand up in a "high-five gesture."

"What are you doing?"

"Isn't that how you seal a deal these with a high- five."

Gracie rolled her eyes but met my high-five with a clap.

CHAPTER 16

I was sitting across a table from Eric at the Blue. He had just arrived, 20 minutes late. Marlene approached with coffee.

"Is it fresh?" Eric dared to ask.

Obviously, Eric had never been to the "Blue" before because no one ever questioned the "freshness" of what Marlene served.

Marlene's eyes narrowed like a cat about to pounce. "Just as fresh as you are," she answered.

Eric laughed taking this as a compliment, but Marlene didn't even smile. She poured out his coffee, and Eric settled into the chair across from me.

"Sorry I'm late," he said, "but that's one of the downsides of being the boss. No one can do anything without you."

I had no idea where Eric worked nor did I want to know.

There was an uncomfortable pause. Eric smoothed his hand over his bald head as if he had hair. I cleared my uncongested throat a few times. Eric finally took the plunge.

"I guess I should get straight to the point. I know you were close to Joan____ "

"Well, I wasn't that close____

"Please, let me finish." He raised his hand like a traffic cop and I wanted to smack him.

"And I was very close to her too," he continued, "But she chose to run off without a word of goodbye or where she was going - nothing."

"Why would she do that?"

He blinked a few times nervously. "She found out I was having an affair. It had been going on for over a year———"

"With Angela?"

"Yes. But the truth is Joan didn't care what I was doing. She even told me she was glad I found someone - made it easier for her to leave me. I never threatened her in any way. I would never do that."

I didn't know if I believed this but I wasn't sure what to say. I decided to change the subject, "I thought you said Angela was coming too."

He shifted in his chair. "She couldn't make it. She got tied up."

For some strange reason, I had a vision of Angela tied to the bedposts with those furry handcuffs I had seen in their bedroom. I immediately blushed and looked down at my coffee.

"Her and Angela had known each other before. In fact, Joan had recommended her for the job. She had been one of Joan's students."

"Really?" I said hoping the sarcasm in my voice was strong enough.

"I mean they weren't friends or anything like that, if that's what you're thinking."

"No." I lied.

"I guess she didn't talk to you about it at all."

"No, I didn't know her well enough for her to talk to me about any problems with her marriage."

"She always held her cards close to her chest. I never really knew what she was thinking. No one knew her well enough for that. She didn't have any close friends and her parents are both dead. I always felt a bit sorry for her."

He was trying to sound genuine, but to me he sounded completely patronizing. He was making Joan sound completely pathetic. Was I being too hard on him? Perhaps I didn't trust any man. Perhaps that's why I haven't had any real long-term relationships.

Marlene intervened holding a coffee pot. "More coffee?"

"No, I'm good," I said.

"Nice place you've got here. I should come more often," said Eric.

I couldn't believe it but by the tone and look on Eric's face, he was flirting with Marlene.

"You're wife used to come in all the time," said Marlene cutting his come-on off at the knees. But her comment struck me as strange. I had never seen Joan at the Blue but I guess we were on different timetables.

"Well, she was always going off on her own to different places."

"Who could blame her," said Marlene with a smile that she reserved for assholes, then sauntered back to the counter.

"I guess people still think of me as the bad guy in all this."

I wasn't sure how to respond. I didn't think he was a "bad" guy. I just didn't like him.

He stood up and now there was an edge to his voice. "I'm sorry I took up your time. I just wanted to be friends, but it's obvious that I'm not welcome here. If you see Joan again, tell her I just want a divorce and be done with it." He threw down a five-dollar bill and stormed off.

I turned to Marlene. "I didn't know Joan came in here."

"She didn't. I just thought I'd throw that at him."

"Maybe we were too hard on him."

"Maybe. We'll see."

Chapter 17

"Your life is turning into a low-rent reality show," said Imogene, taking another gulp of her coffee. She and Gracie were seated at my kitchen table.

"Oh, thanks," I said, "that's a real pick-me-upper."

"Don't get all tied up with yourself. I was just kidding."

"Well, it's not funny."

"We could be the half-priced Kardashians," said Gracie, standing up and slinging her backpack over her shoulder. I noticed she now has a "Geek Goddess" decal sewn next to the marijuana one.

"Make that quarter-priced," I said.

Gracie gave me a second rare hug in the space of only one week.

"Mom, cool your jets. Everything will work out."

"Well, that's an old expression," said Imogene.

"It is?" asked Gracie, wide-eyed with surprise.

Gracie's expression forced me to smile. "Yeah, it was used before you were born."

"Cool."

"So was that," said Imogene, "Way, way before you were born."

"See you later, alligator," Gracie laughed. "Yeah, I know that's old too." She said sauntering out the door.

Imogene and I stared at each other puzzled.

"What's gotten into her?" asked Imogene.

"I dunno but I hope it lasts."

Imogene and I sat in a comfortable silence for a while. Outside of Marlene, she was one of the very few people, I could do that with comfortably. Of course, after a few minutes, my mind started spinning again.

"I wonder what Joan is doing now?" I asked

"Getting crazier."

"She called me to meet her but then she didn't show up. I guess I never really knew her."

"Who knows anybody, really."

"Yeah, I don't even know myself."

Just then my cell went off. I didn't recognize the number or the area code. I put it on speakerphone.

"Hello?"

Bambi's excited voice comes through the speaker. "I just want you to know that I'm here at a coffee shop in Vegas with all the other losers. I just left a Gambler's Anonymous Group meetin' cause I lost all that money I won. That's the bad news."

But guess what? – an hour ago my losin' streak turned into a winnin' one. I met a real cool dude here. His name is John - John Wayne– can you believe that? He's widowed, has grandkids and thinks I'm pretty hot stuff. We're gettin' hitched."

"What?" was all I could answer with.

"I know, I know. It's all happened lickety-split, but what've I got to lose? I'll be stayin' on here a few more days, maybe a couple weeks. Whatever it takes for us to get through the honeymoon and all that. Everythin' okay with you?"

"Well, I___ "

"Don't you worry 'bout a thing, sweetie. Everythin's gonna work out just fine and dandy. You can bet your booty on that. See you later, doll."

The line went dead. Imogene and I stared at each other for a few seconds, stunned by the news.

"John Wayne?" asked Imogene.

CHAPTER 18

It's been almost two weeks since Bambi's last call. I could only assume that she was still honeymooning in Vegas. After I got over the initial shock of her announcement, I felt somewhat relieved but that eventually slid into melancholy. In spite of the ever-present friction between us, I missed her.

I had not seen or heard from Joan. She must be restarting her life elsewhere but the reason for her leaving and coming back is still a mystery to me. I have not seen any sign of Eric or Angela.

One rainy afternoon, Gracie and I had a close conversation in the kitchen. I was making her favorite – grilled cheese sandwiches.

"So how come you never talk about your mom?"

This caught me totally off guard. It was the first time Gracie had ever talked about her grandmother.

"I mean we don't even have any pictures of her," she continued. "Why is that?"

"Granddad got rid of most of them, but I kept a few."

"Really? Can I see them?"

"Sure. But there's just one." I said cutting her freshly grilled sandwich into quarters. "There's a scrapbook in the cupboard over the fridge, it's in there."

Gracie found the scrapbook and opened it to the first page. Pasted on it was an 8 x 10 glossy of her grandmother at 21. It was taken when she was actively seeking work as an actress.

"Wow," said Gracie," biting into the first quarter of her sandwich, "she looks like Kirsten Stewart?"

"Who's that?"

Gracie rolled her eyes at me, which I normally react to with a lecture, but this time, I caught a glimpse of something in her expression I had never seen before, that reminded me of my mom, her grandmother.

"What was she like?"

I took in a deep breath. "She was always striving for something beyond her reach."

"Is that a bad thing?"

"Well, yes and no. I mean it's good to have dreams. It's good to at least try. But her problem was she just couldn't take rejection very well."

"Who can?"

"Nobody I guess, it's something you have to constantly work on and not let it put you down."

"Is there ketchup?"

I thought my answer was very profound and found her question to be a little dismissive.

"There should be some in the fridge."

She grabbed the ketchup from the fridge and pounded the bottom of the almost-empty ketchup bottle a little too forcefully. "Fuck, there's nothing left."

"Just add a little water. And stop using that word around me."

"Sorry, I forgot"

I couldn't believe my ears. She had apologized. "You know, I think I should let you express yourself any way you like, but sometimes I'm not sure what the boundaries are."

"I understand."

"And if you catch me swearing, I'll apologize to you."

"But it doesn't bother me. I mean I hear it all the time. Things are different now, mom. I mean it's not like when you were my age."

"You mean back in the stone age?"

Gracie laughed. "I mean how did you talk to your mom?"

"I didn't really talk to her. I was only nine when..."

I suddenly occurred to me that Gracie knew nothing about her grandmother. Should I tell her everything?

"When she died. You told me that's when she died," said Gracie.

I let out a deep sigh. "That's not exactly true."

"Not exactly? What does that mean?"

"I'm sorry, I told you that because I thought you were too young to know the truth."

"So what's the truth then?" She took a bite out of her sandwich as if knowing the truth would not really affect her.

"Your grandmother was an alcoholic and could not look after me. I was taken away from her when I was nine and your granddad took me in and raised me."

Gracie stopped chewing on her sandwich. Her face softened and her eyes welled up with tears. "That's awful."

"Yes, it was for her and for me."

"Thank God you had granddad."

"Yes, he took good care of me."

Gracie looked back down at the picture. "Do I look like her?"

"Yes, a bit."

"What about my dad? Do you have pictures of him too?"

"Yeah, he's in there too."

Gracie started flipping through the pages until she came across one of me and Matt leaning up against his dad's Ford Taurus, the car in which Gracie was conceived in.

"Is that you?"

"Yes, me and your dad."

"Wow, look at your hair."

"Yes, we wore it like that back then."

"My dad's kind've of cute."

"Yes, he was."

"Do you think you would've married him, if he hadn't died?"

Now was the time to come clean about my arrangement with Matt's family, but somehow I couldn't go that far. I felt Gracie had become much closer to me in this past hour than she had been in a long time. I just couldn't risk losing that.

"I don't know. We were both very young."

"I'm never gonna have kids."

"What?"

"I don't have to if I don't want to."

"No, you certainly don't."

"I wish there was more ketchup."

"Tell you what, I'll go out right now and get some for you. How's that?"

"You would?"

"Yes, just not right at this moment."

"It's okay. I can wait."

***

There's only one more month left on my unemployment checks, and I've used all the money Bambi gave to Gracie.

I've applied everywhere, from housecleaning to Wal-Mart but even those jobs are gone. I'll have to cancel the Internet soon. It's an expense that's not on my basic survival list but yesterday, I discovered a little glow on my bleak horizon. It was a website simply titled "FindYourJob.com." It asked just one question: "What did you enjoy doing as a child?" Apparently the answer to that question, according to this site, would be your ideal job.

All my life I've only thought of jobs as something you did to pay bills. Jobs aren't supposed to be something you like doing. Only rich people get to do jobs they like.

I soon realized I had no idea about what kind of job I would like doing. In fact I had no idea of anything I liked doing. Everything I seemed to do had the word "should" attached to it. But the question was what did I like to do as a child? I had to think long and hard about that one, but then it came to me: My other favorite thing to do was making dolls.

I made up a whole family of dolls who I called the "Waverleys." There was the daughter Susie and the son Jimmy, not twins but miraculously both the same age, and Mr. And Mrs. Waverley, who didn't have first names, but just called each other "Honey."

In my child's mind, and perhaps even in my adult mind now, they were the perfect family. They never had screaming fights and told each other to fuck off, like my parents did, or called each other names like "loser" or "moron."

I made the Waverleys out of old socks I stuffed with even older socks, and I drew their faces on with my mother's makeup. Mrs. Waverley had a large smiling mouth, courtesy of my mother's lipstick "Red Hot Rose" and Mr. Waverly had a mustache made from my "Evening in Paris" eyeliner.

mustache that curled at the ends.

It's been over twenty years since I thought about the Waverleys. But that evening I began sorting through old socks, and anything else I could find, and began making dolls.

Chapter 19

"You all right or somethin'?" asked Gracie picking up one of my freshly minted "dolls," which was created using a bright green sock, from a pair Gracie wore when she was five or six, stretched over a plastic ketchup bottle. It had red button eyes and hair was made out of looped twist ties. It was on top of my other "dolls" piled high on the table.

"Yeah, I guess this all must look a bit strange."

"Yeah, just a bit. Is this my old sock?" She had a look of concern, like she was worried about my sanity.

"Yes, I don't throw anything out. Do you like it?"

She hesitated. "I dunno. It looks a bit weird."

"It's my ketchup doll," I said with a laugh.

Gracie remained somber-faced.

"Hey, Gracie, wassup?" asked Imogene entering the kitchen surprising us both. Her coming in without knocking had never bothered me before but now it did.

"Nuthin." Gracie brushed past her and headed to the exit.

"Ain't teenagers just peachy?" asked Imogene with a sarcastic smirk.

I rolled my eyes in agreement.

Imogene stepped back with her hands up in the air at my doll-making table. "What's all this?"

"I'm making dolls."

"You might just have something here." She said picking up my "ketchup doll" I mean these are weird enough looking to sell."

"Sell them? Where?"

"Online."

"I had to cancel my internet and I don't know anything about doing that."

"I could put them on mine. Listen I started selling stuff on eBay and made hundred bucks last month."

"What stuff?"

"Stuff I pick up here and there, you know garage sales, what people throw away. It's amazing the crap people will buy on eBay. If I can learn how to sell online, so can you."

"I'm just making these dolls for something to do. That's all. It's no big deal. And I don't want to make it one."

"Why you keep doing that?"

"Doing what?"

"Stomping out any new plan for yourself."

"It's not my plan. It's yours. Can you just let me do things my way?"

"Okay, fine."

We sat in strained silence for a moment.

"Seems we don't have anything to talk about anymore."

"It just shows you how boring our lives are."

"Speak for yourself. My life ain't boring."

"Oh yeah? When's the last time you did anything really fun or interesting?" As soon as I said that I regretted it. I knew how hard Imogene struggled to make a good life for herself. "Look, I'm sorry———"

"Sorry? You don't have to be sorry for me. You're the one that's bored, you're the one that hates her life. I'm working towards a law degree. What're you doing? Just sitting there hatin' yourself."

I wanted to know exactly how working at Quick-Trip was working towards a law degree, but I knew that would just be hitting below the belt. Besides there was something, about what she said that was true, in fact, all of it was true.

"You got something to drink around here?"

"No, I drank it all."

"Just as well, I guess."

"Yeah."

"You want me to go?"

I wasn't sure what I wanted so I remained silent. Imogene stood up.

"Okay, I'll go then."

"I didn't say for you to go."

"Then what are you saying?"

"Would you like a coffee?"

"Sure, but let me make it. Your coffee's watered right down until it's just water again."

I smiled. "You mean you've always hated my coffee but still drank it?"

Imogene rinsed out the coffee pot, "The trick is using really cold water to start with."

CHAPTER 20

It's mid-afternoon at The Blue Moon. Marlene and I are the only ones here enjoying the quiet. I'm seated at a café table sipping coffee while Marlene's making me a club sandwich on the house. It's the advantage and disadvantage of living in a small town, everybody knows your business, so everybody knows I've been out of work for a while, especially Marlene, who always has her ear to the ground.

I hate charity. I worked as a volunteer at a soup kitchen once, and I'm ashamed to admit that I felt slightly superior to the people I served. It's much easier for me to give than receive, but now Marlene's feeding me, which is very hard for me to swallow, pun intended.

Marlene sat down with me while I finished her "Join The Club" sandwich.

"I have a little proposition for you," she said, "My dishwasher just quit to have a baby. She'll be gone for a year. I pay a little over minimum if you're interested. It might keep you afloat for a while."

"I'm interested," I said. This wasn't charity, she needed help and I could help. Could things possibly be looking up, just a bit? I'm always so guarded when I start to be hopeful. Hope can be very misleading.

Imogene walked through the door looking a little flushed and anxious. She had recently enrolled in a paralegal night course at a local community college. We've spent less time together because of it.

"I saw you in here while I was driving by," she said. Sorry, if I'm interruptin' somethin.'" She gave both Marlene and me an accusatory look like we'd betrayed her.

"No, we were just having coffee. Marlene just offered me a job here."

"Really? Doing what?" There was a note of condensation in her voice.

"Washing dishes."

Imogene rolled her eyes.

"You have a problem with that?" asked Marlene.

"Who said I had a problem?" said Imogene looking ready for a fight. I'd seen that look on her before, and it's not one you want to push too far.

There was a tense pause, the kind that's just before you light a firecracker.

Marlene backed off. "I'll leave you two ladies to talk while I go practice *bodhicitta*."

I had no idea what *bodhicitta* was but it sounded mystical.

"So it seems you have a problem with me washing dishes in here," I said.

"Yeah, I do. I mean, here I'm tryin' to better myself and you're in here with Marlene, you know, and now you're going to settle for a dishwashing job," she answered looking almost tearful.

"I need a job, Imogene. I'm sorry if it doesn't meet your high standards____"

"Hey, you're talkin' to me, bitch. I live in a trailer park."

When the "b" word is used between Imogene and I, which is usually used by her, a stop sign goes up in our conversation. This time the pause lasted for a good two minutes.

"What's this really about, Imogene?"

"It's about what it's about. You not trying to improve yerself."

"Well, I appreciate your concern but isn't me improving myself my business?"

"Yes, but I thought we were friends."

"We are."

"So, I'm worried about you, just lettin' life keep you down, when are you gonna stop settlin' for crap?"

"Listen, right now I need a job and____"

"Fine, wash dishes all your life, if that's what you want!"

"No, it's not what I want it's____"

"You'll always have some excuse not to better yourself. Well, I'm tired of listenin' to it!" she said, standing up and heading to the door. She turned around to say something, and I caught a glint of tears in her eyes, but she changed her mind and stormed out.

"What is wrong with her?" I asked Marlene who had returned to the table.

"I think she's a bit jealous. When's the last time you called her?"

"I dunno."

"So, it's been a while."

"Yeah, I guess so." I let out a sigh. "The truth is it's just lately I'm finding her really pushy.

"What is she pushing you about?"

"Well, you heard her. I mean right now I can't afford to be choosy about what job I get. I'm just grateful to you about offering me any job. I know she says she's just trying to help, but I don't like being pushed. I'll do things my way, at my own time, and when I'm good and ready to."

I suddenly realized that I was standing up and my fists were clenched like I was ready to slug someone.

"She really hit a soft spot with you," said Marlene.

Just then my cell phone went off. It was Gracie wanting to know if she could invite three of her friends over for a sleepover. That was the last thing I wanted but I owed Gracie some relief.

CHAPTER 21

By the time I got home from The Blue Moon, Gracie's friends were there and the party was in full swing. Music that Gracie called "techno" was thumping from the basement. I closed the basement door, and it muffled the sound, but the bass still managed to vibrate my bones.

I remember listening to loud thumping music when I was their age too. I guess there is something about getting older that makes us turn down the volume. And every generation has their "music" which the former generation can barely tolerate or understand. I grew up loving blues and R&B, but that became disco which was great to dance to but had no real soul or substance. I've gotten into arguments about "rap" music. Even though some of the messages are sexist, homophobic or downright racist, at least some thought has been put into it. It's a jagged and raw poetry.

Just as I was hanging up my coat, Gracie and her three friends emerged from the basement: Amanda with jeans shredded at both knees, Carrie, who's rail thin, with orange spikes streaked through her black hair and finally Carla, who's a little on the plump side but seemed to celebrate that with a bright pink top and huge hoop earrings.

They greeted me in unison with an automated "Hello Mrs. Birdwhistle." even though they knew I wasn't married, and preferred the "Ms." Salutation.

"Can we have some sodas?" asked Gracie from the kitchen fridge, taking out three cans before I could answer.

"Sure that's fine. You want something to eat?"

"We're just gonna order a pizza."

I know Gracie couldn't afford a pizza, and she knew I couldn't either. "I can make something. What would you girls like?"

"Pizza," Gracie insisted.

"Well, I can't afford a pizza right now but___"

"Mom," Gracie said with exasperation punctuated with an eye-roll. "We're all chippin' in."

"Okay, okay," I said joining them in the kitchen. Gracie handed each girl a no-name cola.

"I got some good news today. I got a job."

"Oh yeah? Where?" Gracie asked with guarded interest.

"At the Blue Moon."

"Doing what?" Her face blushed a bit like she was afraid of the answer.

"Washing dishes."

Gracie's face reddened with humiliation. Should I have made up a more acceptable job?

Both Carrie and Amanda looked away covering their smiles, but Carla spoke up tentatively.

"My mom worked there too washing dishes when she first came here."

"Oh, really?" I said grateful for her support.

Carla gave the other girls a sideways glares, "Yeah."

"Whatever," said Gracie, sauntering out of the kitchen. Carrie and Amanda followed her sipping their sodas.

Carla stayed behind. She looked up at me earnestly, "Marlene helped my mom out a lot too."

Before I could say anything, Carla ran to join the other girls.

I was determined to relax in spite of embarrassing Gracie, and the hammering music coming from the basement. I made myself a huge bowl of popcorn, slathered it with cheap margarine, went up to my bedroom, and, since my cable had been cut off, watched my CD of "Bridget Joan's Diary" for the 15th time.

CHAPTER 22

The next morning I made my way down to the kitchen. Bambi was seated at the table having coffee. Surprisingly, I still had the capability of being surprised.

"Mornin'," said Bambi. "I got in late last night, so I didn't want ta wake you. There's a whole gang of girls sleepin' in the basement."

"Gracie had a pizza party last night."

"Good. There's coffee made. And in case yer wonderin' I decided not to get hitched after all," said Bambi

"Oh, that's too bad," I said heading to the coffee. We both knew I didn't really mean that.

"No, it ain't. I found out he hated George Carlin. I mean that was your dad's favorite comedian. I mean I know it's a small thing but it says a lot, don't'cha think?"

"Yeah, I guess it does."

"I mean he's entitled to like who he likes but the truth is I guess I was just lookin' for another man exactly like yer dad, and the truth is there isn't ever gonna be one."

"No, there isn't."

"But that doesn't mean that there ain't, lots of good men out there and when you're ready you'll meet one of 'em."

"You mean "you.""

"No, I mean "you.""

"I'm not looking to meet anyone."

"Oh, yes you are and if you're not you should be."

"Bambi!" screamed Gracie from behind me. "You're back." She rushed into the room to give Bambi a big hug.

"Now, that's what I call a greetin'," said Bambi, standing up to hug her.

CHAPTER 23

My first week on the job as a dishwasher at the Blue started at 5:30 a.m. Monday morning. I didn't really wash dishes. There was a dishwasher that did that. I just cleared tables and put them in the machine. Marlene did everything else, cooking, waiting tables, cleaning. It was amazing how hard she worked. The Blue had three main crowds, early breakfast, lunch and happy hour which lasted until it was over.

After my first day, I offered to wait tables and do the sweeping up. Even though I told Marlene she didn't have to pay me more, she raised my pay to $80.00 bucks a week. That was forty bucks more a week than working at the Quick Pick.

Were things possibly looking up for me?

On my third day on the job, just as I was clearing off my last table for lunch, in walked Uncle Ted minus Cindy.

"Hi Alice. Bambi said I would find you here."

I smiled but I couldn't resist my greeting. "Just trying to earn an honest living."

"Well, good for you."

"Can I get you a coffee or something?" asked Marlene from behind me.

"Yeah, coffee would be great," said Uncle Ted.

"Marlene, this is Uncle Ted, Uncle Ted this is Marlene the owner."

"Owner? Well, nice place you got here," said Uncle Ted reaching out to shake Marlene's hand.

"Thanks. It keeps me out of trouble," said Marlene shaking his hand.

"Oh, that's too bad," said Uncle Ted with a wink.

I couldn't believe Uncle Ted was flirting with a woman closer to his own age and I also couldn't believe Marlene was enjoying it.

"Won't you join us?" I asked Marlene.

"Oh, I'd love to but I have a dentist appointment."

"Yes, and it's almost near closing time," I said.

""Don't worry about that," said Marlene. "You two take all the time you want. You can close up when you're finished, Alice. See ya 'all later."

Uncle Ted slid into a booth and I slid into the other side.

"I was just passing through on my way to Chicago." he began, "I'm on a road trip for the first time in my life, but I'm sure you're not interested in that. I just wanted to stop by and say hello and see how you're doing."

"I'm fine."

"How's Grace?"

"She's doing great. How's Cindy?"

"Oh, we decided to part ways. Truth is she met someone else. Someone younger."

"I'm sorry."

"No need to be. I'm over it." He took a gulp of coffee, but his hand was shaking indicating he wasn't over it. "I'm sorry about Christmas. I said some pretty mean things, which I ain't exactly proud of. So I just wanted to clear the air between us."

He looked genuinely sorry. "Consider it cleared," I said. "I think I said some things too that weren't exactly kind. Christmas brings out the worst in people."

We both laughed.

"How's the money situation?" he asked.

I immediately stopped laughing.

"We're getting by."

"I can help, now that I don't have anyone else to spend my money on."

"Thank you, but like you said I think it's about time I stood on my own."

"It's not for you. It's for Gracie."

"Then I can't stop you from giving her money."

"You're not a failure, Alice. Neither was your dad. I'm the failure."

I couldn't believe what I was hearing. I had never seen Uncle Ted humble himself like that.

At that moment I wanted to hug him, but there was a table separating us, and I had never hugged him before, and I felt embarrassed about doing it. "You're not a failure. You're just missing Cindy."

"Thank you, Alice."

"Well, I'm off to see the __ "

"Why don't you stay for dinner?"

"Thanks, but no thanks. I need to be by myself for a while, but I'm glad we had this talk."

"Me too."

"Maybe I'll swing back this way on my way back."

"Sure. Marlene can make you one of her famous Heartbreak Hamburgers."

"I'd like that."

"I think she would too."

We both knew we weren't talking about hamburgers.

CHAPTER 24

I was just settling into the deepest sleep I had had, in a very long time, when it was interrupted by the loud rat-tat-tat sound of firecrackers going off. In spite of my sleepy state it dawned on me that it wasn't the 4th of July.

The second volley made me fully awake because it was followed by glass crashing.

Things started adding up in my sleep-fogged brain. The glass breaking sound had come from next door, and so had the shots. Someone had shot out Eric's front window. I immediately thought of Joan.

JOAN

CHAPTER 25

My name is Joan Lewis. I'm 48 years old and I lived in Washte, Nebraska. I taught English Literature at the University of Omaha. I've been married to Eric Lewis, a man of great ambition but little success, for over ten years. I'm not sure when his cheating started but if I really wanted to face my suspicions, probably shortly after we were married. What a fool I've been to believe he would ever change but I've changed. In my attempt to harden my feelings, so that his cheating didn't matter, I became a solid mass of hatred.

I've tolerated his philandering and I've supported his failed ideas by investing my hard-earned savings into his businesses, all of which failed, because he started them off too big, with too many employees. His first venture was a moving company which failed after a year, then a work-out gym, then a flooring company, then a pizza take-out parlour. He had one thing in common with all of these diverse businesses, he knew nothing about them and did little research into them beforehand. He believed that hands-on was the best way to learn something, and that I was too "pedantic". I was more surprised that he knew the meaning of that word then offended. Nevertheless, I supported him by handing over my hard-earned savings and start-up money.

I was drawn to him by his very charismatic personality. He was so unlike anyone I'd ever known.

I come from a very conservative and religious family. My father was an accountant, and my mother was a stay-at-home mom, whose biggest adventure was creating the perfect center piece for our Thanksgiving Dinners, which were attended by our only living relative, my Uncle a confirmed bachelor, who told the same boring stories over and over again.

I met Eric curiously enough at the check-out counter at the Quick-Pick, where my neighbor Alice works. I had just bought a stack of frozen dinners and he said that the Salisbury steak was his favorite.

I don't normally talk to strangers but he was so charming and quite handsome, he broke down all my defenses. As my mother once told me "You're not a looker but a booker" which I guess was referring to my love of books.

I was 40 when I met Eric and he was the only long-term relationship I have ever had. To be honest, it was the only relationship I'd ever had period. I'm ashamed to admit it but I was a virgin when I met him.

I've given Eric everything I had and now I have nothing left for myself. His gratitude for what I have done for him was to have an affair with his "assistant". He didn't even try to hide it, which made it all the more infuriating. He thought I would just accept it, that I would just lay down and let him walk all over me like I have always done. What a sad and pathetic fool I was to put up with him for so long. How desperate I must have been. Well, that's not going to happen again. I've been planning for months for a way to get back at him and now I've found the perfect way.

I mentioned my neighbor Alice. I envy her life. She is free and single, with her own home, and a wonderful young daughter. I sat down with her one night and felt so bad when she talked about her situation, her lack of money, and lack of belief in herself. I only wish I had made more of an effort to get to know her, but it's too late now.

For the past few months, my revenge has taken over my every waking thought, even my dreams. I will put Eric through what he put me through. I followed the news reports about him being a prime suspect, but eventually the reports of me missing stopped and he was never arrested. I became a cold case.

That's when I decided to return to Washte and tell Alice what Eric had done to me. I used the words "tried to kill me" in a metaphoric way. He did try to kill me, but I won out in the end.

And now I just want one more parting shot. Literally. I'm standing in front of his house, with my rifle. I haven't used one since I went hunting with my dad.

I'm not drunk or on drugs. It's just that my rage has completely taken over. I'm being very careful. I see that the house is dark and there are no cars in the driveway. So no one's at home. I think I can get four shots in before I can take off.

He just has to pay for what he did to me. For all those years of denying myself for him. He has to pay something.

I raise the rifle to my shoulder and take aim and fire. The shot goes through the living room window. How glorious is the sound of breaking glass.

I stand in shock for a few moments or maybe longer. I see a few lights go on in the surrounding houses. I should get out of here, but I can't move. I'm not sure how long I've stood here standing before I notice someone approaching me. I raised my gun.

CHAPTER 26

Joan looked up at me like she was in another world. Like she didn't recognize me. She raised her gun and aimed it at me.

They say that your life flashes before you just before the moment of death. That was true for me. In that moment all that I had been through in my life up until now flashed through my mind but with incredible detail. It all suddenly made sense for a moment, all the anger I felt towards my mom, and everyone else in my life who had hurt me dissolved and seemed quite meaningless, all the time I had wasted putting myself down, putting others down seemed so pointless. For just a moment I felt this overwhelming sense of love and connection. I wanted to hold onto that moment forever but just as quickly it dissipated and just as quickly I became frozen with fear.

"Stay away," said Joan, the gun she was holding was now trembling.

"I won't come any closer," I said trembling too. "But can we talk?"
"No. It's too late for that now."
I slowly felt my fear ebb away Something had moved over me like a shield. I felt I could withstand anything.

"No, it's not," I said. "It's never too late to start over. I've done it many times," I said amazed by the calmness of my voice.

"Don't give me that bullshit. I've heard them all and they don't mean shit."
I heard someone behind me. I turned to see Gracie and Bambi coming towards me.
"No, stay back," I said to them.

"She's gonna have to shoot me if she shoots you," said Bambi. She turned to Grace and said something I couldn't hear. It made Grace run back into the house.

At that moment I was filled with so much love for Bambi but what a terrible way to experience that love.

I turned back to Joan. "Please, please just put the gun down."

"No. I'm not going to say it again. Get back." She said, raising the gun to her shoulder to take aim.

Bambi moved in front of me.

By the crazed look in Joan's eyes, I felt that she could pull the trigger, that anything, any slight movement by either Bambi or me could make her do that.

I heard the faint sound of police sirens in the distance and closed my eyes. I put my arms around Bambi and then I heard the awful sound of another gunshot.

CHAPTER 27

"Discharging a firearm in certain cities and counties, intentionally or recklessly discharging a firearm, while in or having just exited a motor vehicle, at or in the general direction of any person, dwelling, building, structure occupied motor vehicle, occupied aircraft or inhabited motorhome or camper while in a city of the first class of the county containing a city of the primary or metropolitan class is guilty of a Class IC felony.36...

> *State Capita*
>
> *Lincoln, NE 69509"*

Joan had fired the rifle into the ground and the impact of that threw her off her feet and dislocated her shoulder. Before that happened, Bambi had told Gracie to run into the house and call the police.

Thank God Eric and Angela weren't home. They were both at a Gamer's Convection in Vegas.

With the help of a good lawyer, one that Imogene started working for, Joan did not have to face the mandatory sentence because Eric did not press charges and the district attorney agreed to drop the charges as well if Joan was put on probation for two years and underwent psychiatric counseling.

Angele left Eric shortly after this incident and returned to LA with a guy she met at the Gamer's Convection,

Joan divorced Eric and he left Washte for good, His whereabouts are unknown.

After six months in a psychiatric hospital, Joan moved back into her house and we've become good friends.

Marlene and I worked so well together, she made me a partner in the Blue, and on the side, I sell my dolls,

Imogene helped me create a web page for my dolls which I have entitled Waverly's. Com. Our relationship continues to grow even though we have fights and disagreements. I've learned a lot from her.

Bambi has reconnected with John Wayne, but that's only on Facebook. Even though I've warned her about doing this, they exchange provocative pictures of each other.

This started off with the mystery of Joan's disappearance but there were other more personal mysteries that I've tried to discover the answer to: like what motivates me to do the things I do? I'm sure that's a mystery we would all like answered about ourselves.

Sheriff Carton and I have started dating.

About the Author

Kathleen Martin's first Novel "Penny Maybe" was published in Canada and Germany. She is also a Gemini-nominated writer for film and an award-winning playwright. She lives in Phoenix, Arizona.

Read more at https://www.facebook.com/KathleenMartinauthor.